This book belongs to:

. . . .

Dedicated to Giovanna,
who is so dedicated to stories

—R.M.

To Madeleine & Elliott

—A.R.A.

THIS IS A BORZOI BOOK PUBLISHED BY ALFRED A. KNOPF

Text copyright © 2014 by Roman Milisic
Jacket art and interior illustrations copyright © 2014 by A. Richard Allen

All rights reserved. Published in the United States by Alfred A. Knopf, an imprint of Random House Children's Books, a division of Random House LLC, a Penguin Random House Company, New York. Originally published by HarperCollins, London, in 2014.

Knopf, Borzoi Books, and the colophon are registered trademarks of Random House LLC.

Visit us on the Web! randomhousekids.com
Educators and librarians, for a variety of teaching tools, visit us at RHTeachersLibrarians.com

Library of Congress Cataloging-in-Publication Data
Milisic, Roman.
Apes a-go-go! / by Roman Milisic ; illustrated by A. Richard Allen. — First American edition.
  p. cm.
"Originally published by HarperCollins, London, in 2014"—Copyright page.
Summary: "When the mayor of the tidiest town notices a single flower out of place, Fussy Great Ape offers to help. Unfortunately, he causes a bigger mess in the process. He calls on his other ape friends to help, but their good intentions lead the town into even greater chaos! Can they put this town back together?" —Provided by publisher
ISBN 978-0-553-53363-7 (trade) — ISBN 978-0-553-53364-4 (lib. bdg.) — ISBN 978-0-553-53365-1 (ebook)
[1. Apes—Fiction. 2. Cleanliness—Fiction. 3. City and town life—Fiction. 4. Humorous stories.] I. Allen, A. Richard, illustrator. II. Title.
PZ7.1.M56Ap 2015
[E]—dc23
2014038895

The text of this book is set in 14-point Square Slabserif 711 BT.

MANUFACTURED IN CHINA
July 2015
10 9 8 7 6 5 4 3 2 1

First American Edition

Roman Milisic & A. Richard Allen

APES A-GO-GO!

ALFRED A. KNOPF

New York

Once upon a time, there was a lovely town.
It was so well kept that it was set to win the Tidiest
Town Competition for the third year in a row.

Everything in it was perfect.

Everything, except for one flower, which had grown a little taller than the rest.

"Bah! That pesky flower," grumbled the town's persnickety mayor.

Unfortunately, he trampled the entire flower bed in the process.

"See what you've done, you Fussy Great Ape!" cried the irate mayor.

"Oops!" Fussy Great Ape winced.
"But not to worry—I know just who can fix this."
And before the mayor could say a word, Fussy Great Ape lifted his head,
pounded his chest,
and yodeled,

BOGO! POGO! APES A-GO-GO!

(which is how Great Apes call each other).

Luckily, a passerby at that very moment heard the mayor's complaint.

It was **Fussy Great Ape.**

"Why, all it needs is a little nudge," said Fussy Great Ape, who liked things just so. "I can fix it, Mr. Mayor!"

And, delicately, he did!

Minutes later, who should turn up but **Mucky Great Ape.**
A brilliant gardener, he took one look at the flower bed
and said, "I can fix it, Mr. Mayor!"

Yes, he replanted the flower bed. Unfortunately, he muddied up the whole street in the process.

"GAH! Look at what you've done, you Mucky Great Ape!" barked the mayor from under a mountain of dirt.

"Oh, no!" cried the sorry ape. "But I know who can clean this up in a jiffy."

So now both Great Apes threw back their shoulders, pounded their chests, and hollered,

Sopping Great Ape, who positively *loved* cleaning.
He took one look at the muddy rumpus and said,
"I can fix it, Mr. Mayor!"

And—splish, splosh—
he did . . .

. . . causing a huge
flood in the process.

"Why, you Sopping Great Ape!"
roared the furious mayor,
water pouring from his pockets.

"Yikes!" said Sopping Great Ape.
"But worry not!"

Up went the apes' cry again,

And along came …
Thumping Great Ape.

"What you need is some drain holes,"
he said.

"I can fix that, Mr. Mayor!"

And he did.

Kind of.

"Oh, you Thumping Great Ape!"
wailed the mayor.
"My beautiful town, it looks like
Swiss cheese!"

"No good?" asked the hairy
fellow, who had, after all,
drained off all the water.

In no time at all, the apes were pounding their chests again, and raising the cry,

to summon . . .

Sweeping Great Ape, who knew *exactly* how to get rid of holes.

Swishing and brushing, he got rid of the holes, all right . . .

. . . but unfortunately, he got rid of *everything else,* too!

"ARGHHH! You Sweeping Great Ape!" frothed the enraged mayor.
"My town! Ruined!" Which was as much as you could get from him,
as he was now rolling on the ground, gnashing his teeth.

"Now, let's stay calm, Mr. Mayor," pleaded Sweeping Great Ape, in a bit of a panic. "There is one last solution."

And together, all the Great Apes lifted their heads, pounded their chests, and called at the tops of their voices,

"BOGO! POGO!

And who should turn up
but **Baking Great Ape.**

"Well now, dears, I'm sure I can fix this!"
Baking Great Ape smiled, for she had some
experience in fixing disasters.

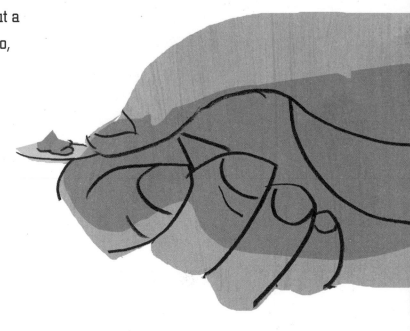

Then she baked a huge cake and put a
little piece in front of the mayor, who,
through his tears, took a nibble.

"*Mmm.*"

And then a
little more.

"Yum."

All the townsfolk and all the Great
Apes had a slice, too. Someone
brought balloons. And, you know,
people really started to enjoy
themselves.

Meanwhile, the Great Apes were doing a fine job of putting things back together; maybe not quite as perfectly as before, but with plenty of charm.

At that moment, the mayor realized that maybe there was more to life than a perfect town. Like warm cake and good friends. He may not have the Tidiest Town any longer, but it just might be the happiest.

"Well, that was delicious," said the mayor as he polished off the final crumb and folded his napkin neatly. "But who's going to clean up all these plates?"

"Allow me, Mr. Mayor!" said **Smashing Great Ape**, who was near at hand.

The mayor thought about it for a moment.

"On second thought," he said,
"I think I'll do it myself."

And he did.